I'm a Hop Hop Hop Hoppity Frog

Story by Lawrence Northey
Illustrations by Julie Northey

Stoddart Kids

Published in Canada in 2002 by
Stoddart Kids,
a division of Stoddart Publishing Co. Limited
895 Don Mills Road, 400-2 Park Centre, Toronto, Ontario M3C 1W3

Published in the United States in 2002 by
Stoddart Kids
a division of Stoddart Publishing Co. Limited
PMB 128, 4500 Witmer Estates, Niagara Falls, New York 14305-1386

www.stoddartkids.com

To order Stoddart Kids books please contact General Distribution Services
In Canada Tel. (416) 213-1919 FAX (416) 213-1917
Email cservice@genpub.com
In the United States Toll-free tel. 1-800-805-1083 Toll-free FAX 1-800-481-6207
Email gdsinc@genpub.com

06 05 04 03 02   1 2 3 4 5

National Library of Canada Cataloguing in Publication data

Northey, Lawrence, 1952–
I'm a hop hop hoppity frog

ISBN 0-7737-3335-3

I. Northey, Julie, 1956– II. Title.

PS8577.O688I42 2002   jC813'.6   C2001-902926-8
PZ7.N816Im 2002

THE CANADA COUNCIL | LE CONSEIL DES ARTS
FOR THE ARTS | DU CANADA
SINCE 1957 | DEPUIS 1957

*We acknowledge for their financial support of our
publishing program the Canada Council, the Ontario Arts
Council, and the Government of Canada through the
Book Publishing Industry Development Program (BPIDP).*

Printed and bound in Hong Kong, China
by Book Art Inc., Toronto

This book is dedicated
to all the delightfully active children
we have worked with and know,
and to our son, Ono,
our truest inspiration and shining light.

— JULIE AND LAWRENCE NORTHEY

I'm a hop hop hoppity frog,

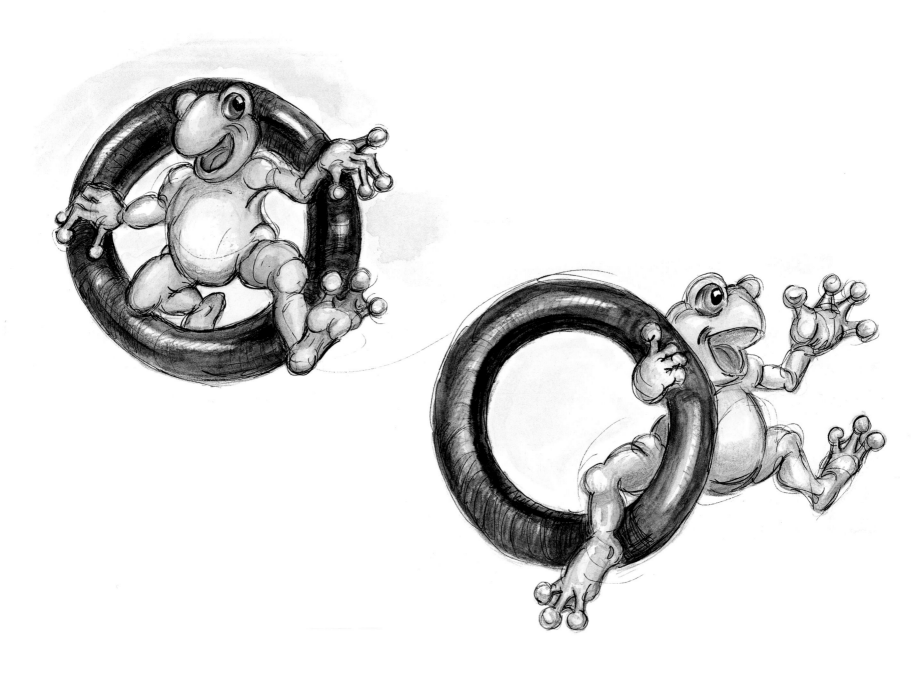

I'm a hop hop hoppity frog.

I love to hop,

It's hard to stop!

I'm a hop hop hoppity frog.

I have to play and sing,
　　And dancing is my thing,
　　　　　I'm a real be-bopper,
　　　　　　a get down hopper!

I'm a hop hop hoppity frog.

In the summertime,
When the weather's fine,

I swim and swing and jog.

I'm a hop hop hoppity frog,
I'm a hop hop hoppity frog.

I love to hop,

It's hard to stop!

I'm a hop hop hoppity frog.

I love to ride around,

Jump up . . .

. . . jump down.

Shake it

left . . .

. . . shake it right.

Run back and forth,

South to north,

Morning . . .

. . . until night.

I'm a hop

hop

hoppity frog,

I'm a hop hop hoppity frog.

I love to hop,

It's hard to stop!

I'm a hop hop hoppity frog.

I'll say it again,
From beginning to end,

I'm a hop hop hoppity,
Hop — don't stoppity —
A hop hop hoppity frog.
Yeah!